P.I. DIARIES

Joseph Mullen

ISBN: 978-0-692-10037-0

Names, characters, and places have been fictionalized
in some cases to protect individuals' true identities.

Printed by Amazon.com

First Print Edition, 2018

Mullen Productions
1706 Tower Drive, Edgewater, NJ 07020

Mullen Productions
jt@jtmullencompany.com
http://www.jtmullencompany.com

To my son Thomas

He left us too soon.
He was my right hand and my soulmate.

-His Dad

Credits

Editors: Susan Cannon, Jen Harris, Victoria Shannon
Photographers: Chase Cabral, Stuart Heidmann, Karen Shapiro
Graphic Design: Samantha Langford
Development: Suzanne Kramer Mullen, Ken Petti

I came from a Bronx walk-up.

*Within a few decades
I helped the families of
four Presidents,
three Prime Ministers
and a King.*

Joe

CONTENTS

PREFACE

Immerse yourself in New York City's underworld of secrets, lies, and sexy dish, inspired by the real-life investigations of Bronx-born Joseph Mullen, New York's most famous shamus.

In **_P.I. Diaries_**, Mullen writes with compendious style and dry wit, turning his highbrow sleuthing into an intriguing, fictionalized scrapbook narrative.

During his illustrious half-century career as a renowned P.I., Mullen's sizzling-hot clientele was wowed by his epic brand of investigative brilliance, not to mention his good looks and dashing style—style that easily matched Bogart's, Sam Spade.

In Mullen's early years, he was Judy Garland's bodyguard. Throughout the decades, he worked countless cases involving famous clients like Johnny Carson and Donald Trump. With apparent ease, he tracked down the secret love child of Fidel Castro who was hiding out in Miami.

Many cases played out on the national and international stages. Mullen was a central figure who investigated the FBI's notorious ABSCAM sting, solving the case in only four days.

He broke the Wall Street yuppie insider-trading scandal wide open, and he saved the reputation of global banking icon Edmond Safra by exposing an international smear campaign against him by one of the world's largest financial institutions—American Express.

Combined with street savvy and common sense, it was axiomatic that if Joe Mullen were on a case, the job would get done… bada bing, bada boom. Mullen seemingly possessed the ability to perform a psychological autopsy on those he investigated. His relentless drive and brilliant imagination, his humor, charm, and glamorous gumshoe character garnered him not only a golden clientele but more props and press in both print and on TV than any other private investigator throughout the years.

Enhancing his esteem further, Mullen is also a family man, a compassionate advocate for child-related charities, and, for many years, an avid runner and amateur boxer. These blended qualities will keep you eating up every word

ABSCAM

In 2013, Hollywood came out with a black comedy called *American Hustle*. This film was loosely based on the famous ABSCAM operation of 1979 involving political corruption and bribery.

ABSCAM started for me one quiet Saturday morning.

I got a call from a friend of mine—a major Korean War hero who had become a formative U.S. congressman. He told me about some men he had recently met with who "smelled" bad and he needed me to check them out. He suspected they were con men or government agents pretending to work for an Arab company called Abdul Enterprises. He gave me the address of a small Georgian mansion in a quiet neighborhood of Washington, D.C., and my brief, albeit crucial, involvement in the ABSCAM caper began.

This occurred way before computers, and in retrospect, I can say that my m.o. then was to operate with such speed as to get leading information—just as fast as if I were hitting the return key on a Google search. One of my sources was the Cole Directory. This directory was tops in data management and showed addresses and phone numbers covering the bulk of America. Using the contact information I got from Cole, I made cleverly scripted ruse calls to numerous neighbors of the subject's address to obtain information.

I only made my calls before dinnertime, so as not to annoy anyone. I was told the townhouse looked like a movie set all day long, but after 6 p.m. everyone vanished. As one difficult conversation after another led nowhere, I came upon one female neighbor who turned out to be quite an observant fashion plate. She recalled being impressed that the men were all wearing Flagg Brothers shoes.

It took me four days to deduce that the men must have been government agents.

I called the congressman and told him what I had found. "That's exactly what I suspected," he remarked. Little did I know that what I had just uncovered was a major sting operation that ultimately brought down senators and other prominent political figures. Within a year, I was testifying before a grand jury in Brooklyn. I took the Fifth, and U.S. District Attorney Tom Puccio congratulated me on my investigative services. After the trial, Murray Kempton wrote a very positive story in the *New York Post* about the congressman and me. I ended up working on the Astor case and many other top investigations for Tom Puccio as a result.

Some years later, I ran into one of the FBI agents involved in ABSCAM in an Irish bar on West 57th Street. We didn't agree on much of anything in that chance meeting, and I told him, "ABSCAM clearly wasn't your finest hour, sir."

I maintain today that the congressman was the real hero in the whole affair.

ALMOST FARGO

I met a man in the dead of winter who looked like a cross between Burl Ives and John Candy. He owned a three-generation-old family business in Lower Manhattan, which he successfully expanded into the other New York boroughs. His life was seemingly sweet, until one day it wasn't.

He hired me to uncover his wife's infidelity and betrayal. She had apparently fallen back in love with an old flame while attending a college reunion. It's a scenario I've seen time and again in my long career as a P.I.

I made my daughter and her boyfriend the principal investigators in the case. They followed our subject everywhere around the city, all the way up to Lake George in the New York Adirondacks. While on her tail for more than four hours, the subject suddenly disappeared.

My investigators continued their search and found evidence of our subject's car on the freshly fallen snow. (My daughter, taking her cue from dear pops, had cleverly knife-marked the subject's tire with a large "Z.") These tracks led them to the frozen lake, and then onto the ice of the frozen lake. I was following them in my car. We honestly didn't expect to find that our subject's new lover lived in the middle of the lake. There were small islands everywhere. It was just a matter of then figuring out which one he called home.

During the ensuing time, we staked out the lovebirds to get the evidence we needed for our client. We had to do our work by car, on and off the ice, in the frigid temps. You could drown if you went through the ice, which created a hell of a lot of anxiety for us. There were numerous cars parked near the small islands in the center of the lake because of all the ice-fishing activity. A few locals had built a small four-by-five-foot shack and would fish from the inside, using heaters and drinking booze. Of course, the ice fishermen were outraged that we were driving all around and kept scolding us for scaring off their fish. It was an arduous, less-than-comfortable task as the homes had no house numbers and everything looked the same, not to mention we were nervous about falling through the damn ice.

Imagine, here we were, these New York private investigators from the concrete jungle up in this sylvan paradise freezing our asses off, slipping around like crazy. We kept hearing ice crack around us and were concerned that it was thin to hold our weight, so we just kept moving.

Finally, we had our moment. We saw the subject's car parked on the ice near a small island with a little cabin and a dock. We observed the male subject coming out of the cabin. He had a rod which had buckets on each end. It looked like a Norman Rockwell Christmas card. Our subject, the client's wife, was standing at the door watching him. Her boyfriend went to the foot of the dock. It was quite a scene. I was waiting for Native Americans to appear...this was undoubtedly not the modern-day Bronx.

The subject came out, and we started snapping photos. We got on the horn with our client who was nearing the lake, and we gave him specific directions to where he could drive onto the lake to join us. He had the subpoena for his wife, and he kept nervously repeating, "She is a champion skier! She'll ski off the ice! No one will be able to keep up with her!"

At this point, we had four investigators, including the photographer, in our party. We had to stay overnight to prove adultery and to execute service of the divorce. My client parked his car on the ice, then sat in my car.

During the night, we observed a great deal of festivity. The fishermen were drinking and fishing and having a great time. Our client created his own party by bringing a bottle of liquor into my car to keep us warm. Mind you, he weighed an excess of 275 pounds and was smoking cigarettes nonstop. We caught him falling asleep, burning holes through his overcoat and shirt. He even singed the hair on his chest.

Throughout the night the noise from the ice crackling below never stopped, and we were afraid to keep our engines going. It was intense.

The next morning, we observed our subject and her lover outside of the cabin. We saw the subject move her car onto the ice. Our client, who was still drunk, had warned us to serve the papers to her before she drove off. He began yelling at us that we'd surely lose her since she was an Olympic skiing champion and was in great physical shape. He then suddenly fumbled to his car and took off.

My investigators raced behind our out-of-control client, who was driving towards the boyfriend's cabin. Two of the investigators jumped out of their cars to serve the subject and her lover while the photographer was rapidly snapping photos of the scene. The boyfriend then took out his camera and started taking shots of the investigators who were taking pictures of him! It was mayhem. There was a lot of screaming: from the subject, her boyfriend—even the fishermen on the lake, whose fishing lines we'd accidentally broken during our car chase.

After we had served the subject the papers, the client began to speed off the ice to leave Lake George. We realized that he was driving in the wrong direction. He didn't know that there were specific exits to get off the ice so as not to hit the unfrozen edges of the lake. We frantically drove to catch up with him, yelling at him from our windows. All four cars lost control. With the sudden stepping on the brakes, the cars were spinning in figure eights, barely avoiding hitting one another. It was utterly madcap and looked like something straight out of a Keystone Cops movie.

Later on, we all met at the local restaurant. Our client thanked us for our services just as we were observing the burn marks on his shirt and coat. We were all tired and had a hysterical laugh because it looked like he had been shot several times in the chest. Before we left for the city, we thought it wise to get a room for our dear, imbibing client so he could sleep it all off. Mind you...a nonsmoking room!

THE AMBASSADOR AND THE TENANT

There's a trendy restaurant on Madison Avenue near 70th Street that draws a socialite crowd—or at least the owners think it does. Nighttime brings in young women looking to meet wealthy older men. The dessert menu even lists the telephone number to Page Six just in case a star stumbles into the place.

A client of mine who was an Ambassador called one day and told me the oddest, most interesting story. It reminded me of a Woody Allen film, minus the ironic humor.

The Ambassador, who was in his 70's and had five grandchildren, met an old friend at this Madison Avenue restaurant for a few drinks. His friend had recently lost his wife of 40 years and needed a shoulder to lean on. They sat at a table near the bar, and an attractive young woman was sitting alone at a table next to them. She had two traveling bags with her, designer, naturally. This was not that unusual as it was a Friday summer evening when all roads lead to the Hamptons and Fire Island. After the Ambassador's friend left and he was paying the check, the young woman appeared at his table.

It should be noted that the Ambassador, while handsome, was a white-haired gentleman, and the woman, who introduced herself as Jill, was at most the same age as his youngest daughter.

It wasn't long before she was telling him her sob story. She explained that she had moved to New York City two weeks earlier to stay with the "love of her life," whom she had recently met at the Beverly Hills Hotel in Los Angeles. He had invited her to his Greenwich Village apartment. Within only a few days, however, their honeymoon was over. His wife showed up unannounced.

Jill said she had rented storage space on the West Side for her a collection of art, clothing, and furniture. (She didn't travel light.) She was now staying in small, inexpensive hotels. Though she never talked about money with the Ambassador, she did say it was hard to get a job when you don't have an address. She claimed to be on a waiting list for a one- bedroom apartment on the Upper West Side.

Without thinking it through, the compassionate Ambassador told her he had an eight-room apartment on Park Avenue and offered her a place for a few days to help her. He said it would need to be short-term because his daughters and grandchildren would be arriving to stay later in the month.

Jill went home with the Ambassador, and he gave her a bedroom off the kitchen where his late wife's maid previously lived. Within 24 hours she was as comfortable as the maid had been. The second day, he knocked on her bedroom door to ask if she needed anything. Jill opened the door, and to his surprise, he saw she had already decorated the walls with photos of her mother and her dog and a painting. He didn't recognize the room. By the end of the week, his maid called him at his Rockefeller Center office to report that the telephone company had just been there to install a new line for Jill in the bedroom.

When the Ambassador went home that night, his doorman gave him his mail. It included mail for her, too. Now he was concerned. He didn't recall adopting her! He approached her and told her she had to leave. "Please understand, my family is coming soon, and we're going to Italy where we have a second home. You have to go before they arrive," he said.

Well, travel day came and went, and she hadn't left. The Ambassador called his maid from Rome and asked if Jill was gone. "No, she had the gall to have a party here last night with her friends!" she said. "What friends?" asked the Ambassador.

The Ambassador then called his attorney. His attorney explained, "You have a problem, sir. Jill has been there more than thirty days, and she receives mail and telephone services. These facts qualify her as a tenant."

The Ambassador got his son, also an attorney, to speak with Jill, and he saw her true colors come out. She knew the New York law, and she knew she was now a legal tenant on Park Avenue. This cunning woman was not going anywhere!

This is where I came in. We got lucky. Within ten minutes our computer research told us that "Jill" had a warrant out for her arrest in California for cashing fraudulent checks, and she had been using an elderly person's credit card. What a surprise! The 19th Precinct was eager to get rid of Jill, bags and all. I wondered how her dog photo would look in her jail cell?

I had a friend for life in the Ambassador!

AMERICAN HERO

At one time, Mario Biaggi was the most decorated police officer in America. His second career was as a member of Congress. He represented the Bronx, Riverdale, Yonkers, and Queens. He was there to fight for the "little people," and I'm not talking about the ones from *The Wizard of Oz*. Biaggi passionately championed the Irish, Jews, Italians, blacks, and Hispanics: anyone who needed help and didn't get a fair shake in society. He easily won re-election nine times.

Like others before him, however, he got involved in the political fallout from the Wedtech Corp. corruption scandal, which resulted in his resignation from Congress.

Mario was my best friend for many years. I look back proudly at his many accomplishments, including his championing of the physically challenged, the elderly, and the Washington, D.C., Police Memorial, among others. He was the uncrowned King of the Irish, as the British government once acknowledged.

I remember one time when we were having lunch in our favorite Irish watering hole, Kennedy's, on West 57th Street. As usual, Mario drank a non-alcoholic beer, or maybe a virgin mixed drink that day. (Many of his companions never knew he didn't drink, thanks to the sharp bartender who kept his secret.) He was in his mid-70's, still handsome, and walking with two canes. (As a young police officer, he had saved a young woman's life when she lost control of her horse on the West Side of New York. Mario ran the horse down and hung on to the horse's neck while it was bucking violently. The damage to Mario's legs was crippling later in life.)

As we got into my car after lunch, we heard an elderly woman screaming. A thief had stolen her pocketbook. I was already sitting behind the wheel of the car while Mario was entering the passenger side, which was open to the street. As the young thief was running down the street with the woman's bag, Mario quickly turned around and threw one of his canes, and then the other, at the thug. Then, to my surprise, he leaped the kid, unfortunately missing him. Here he was in his 70's, still taking physical risks. (He had been wounded ten times in the line of duty and had received 28 honors, including the police department's highest award.)

By the time I got out of the car, the kid was out of sight. I stood over Mario who was now flat on his back. We stared at one another and just started laughing. I said, "Always a cop." That's who Mario was. This incident demonstrated his true grit and what a great man he was.

We always kept the Irish pubs happy. Another time we were having a hamburger at D.J. Reynolds, also on 57th Street. On this day, Mario came with his driver, who had spent time in prison and whom Mario had given a job. His driver was very protective and never wanted Mario to have to walk too far, so we sat in his view. Suddenly the driver rushed in very upset. He had just heard news on the radio and said out loud, "They indicted you, Mario!" Mario grabbed both my hands and almost crushed them. He looked into my eyes and said, "Now I need you, Joe. Those sons of bitches..." He appeared down and out for only about 30 seconds and then he was ready for the fight! We threw down our money for lunch and started toward the car. Halfway out of the restaurant, a middle-aged Irish woman yelled out, "Congressman...we need your help! They're throwing my 70-year-old mother out of her Bronx apartment." I put my hand up and said, "Please, not today." Mario put my hand down and asked if I had a pen and paper. I reached for some "Irish stationery"—a bar napkin—from the bartender. Mario then sat down with this upset woman. I stood in the corner completely inspired and in awe. It was one of the worst days in Mario's life, and yet here he was helping a stranger. Who would do this?

When we finally exited the pub, Mario's driver held the door open and was crying for him.

I was shocked.

During the time of his trial, Mario dragged his weak legs to Mount Sinai, where my daughter Pam was recovering from a brain operation. He sat and held her hands. This was also who Mario was.

Like the song says, "He Ain't Heavy, He's My Brother." I miss him.

BEDSIDE MANNERISMS

As is the norm, it started with a call from a divorce attorney. This attorney was also a religious leader in Brooklyn. The surprise was that the client he'd introduced me to was an actress and model, who'd recently been on the cover of a popular skin magazine. I thought to myself; *there is a God.*

That day, this beautiful woman was unable to meet me at her attorney's office for our first meeting, as she was doing PR for her latest movie role. She asked that I instead come to her place to go over the details of her pending divorce before she left for her appointment.

I went home to change into my best suit, shirt, and tie. At a time like this, a Bronx boy wants to look his best.

I entered her apartment, and she showed me into her bedroom. Her shoes were all over the floor. Her dresses were thrown over the doors, on chairs and the bed. She was getting ready to go in front of the cameras at the movie opening. While she was speaking with me, I was taking notes on my yellow pad.

She then disappeared into the bathroom while continuing to tell me about her husband, a well-known movie star and a bit of a playboy himself. She came out of the bathroom, standing in front of me, wearing a bra and panties. That was it. I was still taking notes, and at this point, I kept my eyes down and spontaneously wrote, *I am not going to get paid for this case.*

She went back and forth to the bathroom, and again walked out, this time entirely nude and still talking. I thought to myself; *I wasted money on the skin magazine.*

I had my son Tom follow her husband, his brother, and another European actor who played macho characters in numerous movies.

One night, Tom was at a bar in Montreal some five feet away from these men. They were loaded. At a certain point late in the evening, Tom held the elevator door open for our client's husband, who was so drunk that he could only crawl into the elevator. He asked my son if he was hotel security, and Tom replied that he was.

Tom was then invited to join the men in their suite to party.

A few days later, the local papers reported that a significant Irish movie star had a heart attack and was hospitalized at an East Side New York City hospital.

Our client didn't believe that her husband had a heart attack, and instead, she told us, he must have done too much cocaine on top of being drunk, which surely must have caused his heart rate to accelerate.

The client wanted me to serve her husband the subpoena while he was in the hospital. I questioned whether this would be a good idea, but she insisted. We took a cab ride together to see him. The actress had a scarf on to obscure her famous face. I was familiar with the hospital, so I guided her up a back stairwell to the cardiac unit. We were lurking some 20 feet away from her husband's room when the client said she wanted to speak with her husband before I served him the papers. I suggested that I should go in first to see if he was okay.

I had brought undercover supplies with me, so I could dress like a doctor. I threw on a medical coat and went to his room. It was risky as the nurse's station was just down the hall. As I entered, I observed that the subject was hooked up to all kinds of tubes and machines. I picked up his medical chart, and he remarked that I was holding it upside down. I responded that I was joking around with him, then pretended to read it. I left the room and, on my way, out said to him that I hoped he'd feel better.

I went back to the stairwell where I found my client smoking a cigarette. I told her how sick her husband must be, considering all the wires and tubes, and I suggested we not bother him at this time. She agreed but insisted that she should visit with him quickly before we left.

She slipped into his room without anyone seeing her. After a few minutes, I heard alarms go off and realized something terrible was going on. I watched as four nurses frantically ran down the hallway. I imagined the subject must have had heart failure when he saw his stunning wife enter his room.

Suddenly, my client was back by my side and told me that we should leave the hospital immediately.

I asked what happened and she nervously replied that she had merely kissed her husband, and that had caused the alarm system to go off.

The next day, a local gossip columnist wrote a piece that said something about a star having sex in the cardiac unit of an East Side New York City hospital while hooked up to machines.

Thank God the hospital was not a Catholic hospital. The nurses would have been nuns, and they would've been the ones having the heart attacks.

THE BODYGUARDS

When you think of a bodyguard, you think of the Secret Service or some handsome suit surrounding a celebrity, like in the movie *The Bodyguard*, starring Whitney Houston and Kevin Costner. As a private investigator, I had my share of bodyguard assignments, and I can tell you that film was not a realistic portrayal of the life of a true bodyguard. You never leave your client unprotected.

On Dec. 4, 1992, a newspaper wrote that one of the best bodyguards in the industry was Bob Foti. They also quoted in the article another great bodyguard: "...Joseph Mullen, who was a bodyguard for Judy Garland, Mike Wallace, Walter Cronkite, Anthony Quinn, and David Susskind."

I was hired by CBS to protect Walter Cronkite because the FBI had informed the network that there was a threat against Cronkite, as well as Johnny Carson. (I never told CBS that I had been Carson's secret private investigator when he was in New York.) I assigned one of my investigators, who was a weightlifter, to drive us in Cronkite's car. My investigator kept a pistol, and a shotgun stashed in the car at all times. We used the service entrances when driving Cronkite to CBS or his home.

In one instance, we were escorting Cronkite to Florida during the elections. Because Cronkite had considerable clout, I was able to call ahead and arrange with the local police to give us temporary gun licenses to carry while in Florida. On the last day of our assignment, three of my men were invited by Mrs. Cronkite to have a beautiful dinner at their home.

CBS hired us again to help Mike Wallace. Wallace had received an envelope from a Brooklyn address, and within was a piece of paper that said, "Jew Hater," along with a bloodied napkin. I told Wallace I was going to the local post office to speak with the postal inspectors about the envelope. (Postal inspectors are Class A detectives.) I investigated further, and I found out that a young boy, who was in bed with an infection after stepping on a rusty nail, had a father who didn't like Mike Wallace. The father fed false information to his son and gave him stamps, paper, and an envelope to pull the prank.

In discovering this, I told Wallace he no longer needed a bodyguard. The kid needed a babysitter, and his dad needed a punch in the nose!

In another case, Gina Lollobrigida hired us. At the time, she was a very sexy woman in her 60's. I asked one of my weightlifting investigators to protect her, and she later remarked that he was "built like a Russian tank." She appreciated his physical presence and flirted with him the entire time he protected her.

Many celebrities and high-profile families have been known to fall in love with their bodyguards. Patty Hearst was one example, and going back through my history lessons, Catherine the Great took several lovers from her Royal Guard.

CAR SERVICE

There are many large, established law firms and investment banks in New York City that work 24 hours a day.

Since the world functions on many different time zones, these types of companies make the long working hours bearable for their employees by offering high-end meal deliveries to the office as well as daily, individual car service to and from work. The firms also provide their employees amazing bonuses at the end of each year.

It was not unusual that these employees would work late into the night, often finishing as late as 2 or 3 a.m. The streets would be lined with designated cars assigned to each employee. Some employees would go home, while others would go out to the local bars.

We worked on cases for several of these firms, and we discovered that there were employees who wanted more than the offered perks and benefits. They wanted the lion's share of the profits.

A Wall Street law firm hired us to investigate three of their stockbrokers. These men weren't assigned to work with one another, nor did they even seem to hang out together at the office.

Our client informed us that a driver had confessed that one of these young employees had given him a stock tip while blabbering drunk. We questioned the driver, who then gave us the home address of the stockbroker in question.

One evening my daughter Bonnie, who was a principal investigator on the case, followed this subject by motorcycle to a local bar that he frequented. She arrived ahead of him, put an extra chair at a table, pretending she was sitting with some friends. After he arrived, she struck up a conversation with him, getting him to sit down with her. She was carrying the *Wall Street Journal* and attempted a discussion about the stock market. He was sober and mute.

Another night, while surveilling the same subject, she witnessed him coming out of his apartment carrying a bag of garbage. He took the trash across the street and threw it into a city trash can, which she captured on film.

My daughter went through all the rubbish, found the bag, and discovered a deposit slip for eight thousand dollars as well as his salary check.

It turned out that the check, made out to cash, was from one of the other two employees: one of his partners in crime.

We informed the law firm. After putting this employee under questioning and a certain amount of duress, the subject easily gave up the other two employees.

P.S. The movie *Wall Street* had characters who rode motorcycles in scenarios similar to our cases. Maybe the film producers read our complaint filed in federal court and emulated us for effect.

THE DAY THE DUKE RAN

I lived at Tower 53 off Sixth Avenue in New York City. I had two special friends in the building: Suzanne, who later became my wife, and one of the finest comedic mimics in the world, David Frye.

I was working from my home office on a Saturday when a call came in. The voice sounded like Walter Cronkite, and I said, "Is that you, David?" He laughed and told me he was down in the bar at the 21 Club with a great group and that I needed to come down. "Phyllis Diller is here. Johnny Carson, Ed McMahon—and John Wayne is just walking in now."

He then started to yell at me to get down there. At this point, I had been secretly working with Johnny Carson and his attorney Henry Bushkin. I said to David, "Carson may be annoyed that you know that I know him." Johnny was weird about those things, but David handed the phone over to Carson, who also yelled for me to get down there. I could tell that they were all pretty loaded. I agreed to go and headed on over. The 21 Club was just a few blocks away.

I arrived, and indeed Duke was there. David, who was very short, kept asking Duke, "How tall were you when you were young?" and Duke would say, "Six-foot-four." He kept asking every ten minutes. It was painful. Finally, the bartender said, "Do you want a six-four instead of wine?" It became a joke. Wayne said out loud, "David Frye is somewhat shorter than six-four," and laughed.

We were all drinking by then, and I needed to hit the men's room. Duke followed me. There we were, standing in the men's room when the door suddenly swung open. Phyllis Diller came rushing in holding her dress up. "The ladies' room is very crowded," she screeched with that voice and laugh of hers. Duke and I left the men's room quickly, laughing all the way back to the bar.

Later we sat down at a table near the bar and Phyllis said, "I'm surprised we can hear the rain outside from down here." David looked at Duke. Duke looked at the table. There were only two ice buckets where there had initially been three.

Johnny had put the third one under the table, and he was...well, you get it.

As David Frye and I were walking home, he said to me, "Never tell anyone what happened today." Well, they're all gone now but me. All I can say is that it was an amazing day that I will never forget. Incidentally, my special little dog is named Duke after John Wayne. He was a great guy.

EDMOND SAFRA VS. AMERICAN EXPRESS

In the late 1980s, one of New York's top attorneys hired my firm on behalf of his client Edmond Safra, the founder, and owner of the Republic National Bank.

The case revolved around someone, or perhaps a group of people, trying to ruin the reputation of this international banker. Damaging stories linking Safra to the CIA, the Iran-Contra scandal and, most seriously, to South American drug trafficking began appearing in newspapers and periodicals all over the world.

Edmond Safra had sold his private-banking concern to American Express and agreed not to compete with them for three years. But the suspicion was that Safra would violate that pact and become a rival.

The story became a 500-page bestseller entitled *Vendetta,* written by the author of *Barbarians at the Gate,* Bryan Burrough. *Vendetta* highlighted the J.T. Mullen Company and made many references about the Mullen family of investigators helping with surveillance that would ultimately break the case.

Even my 6-year-old granddaughter, Lizzie, was once with her mother Bonnie when they kept surveillance at the home of an American Express vice president. I remember hearing my granddaughter's excited voice: "Poppy, I saw the subject, I know what she looks like!"

My son Tom spent so much time keeping surveillance at the American Express headquarters on Wall Street that he got friendly with the hot dog vendor stationed near the entrance. Some of the American Express employees bought hot dogs from Tom as he kept his cover standing with the vendor.

Another one of our investigators, Mike Kohut, wrote a book full of notes over many uncomfortable months on his stakeout of a mystery man named Greco on Staten Island. Greco appeared to be the skunk leaking the smelly lies to the press. Kohut used a mirror in the back seat of his vehicle, all the while lying down so his car would appear empty while he surveilled Greco's movements. One day, Greco came out of his Staten Island home dressed in a suit and tie, got into his vehicle, and headed towards the Verrazano-Narrows Bridge. Kohut followed and began singing over his cell phone "Coming to America" as he headed toward Manhattan. That was our cue, and all of our investigators rushed to the American Express headquarters.

I called the attorney and Mr. Safra to alert them that surveillance was at the "beginning of the finale." One of our men took the photo of the subject sitting in his car (in front of the American Express building) receiving an envelope from a VP of American Express.

Safra's attorney had hired private investigators all over the world before bringing in the J.T. Mullen Company. We were the last private investigators hired, and we broke the case wide open.

ELLIS ISLAND MEDAL OF HONOR

In 1999, I was the recipient of the Ellis Island Medal of Honor. The award is bestowed on 100 people annually. To qualify for the honor, one must be an American citizen who has distinguished him or herself within their ethnic group, while exemplifying the values of the American way of life.

William Denis Fugazy and Congressman Mario Biaggi nominated me for this prestigious award.

I have always had a passion for protecting the innocent children of this world. It began when I became the proud father of my daughter at the age of 20 and, shortly after that, the father of three sons and another daughter. Later on, I became the grandfather of 14 grandchildren (seven boys and seven girls).

In the 1980s, I was doing a bodyguard job for Frank Perdue, the "King" of the Purdue Chicken family business. One Thanksgiving holiday, Mayor Ed Koch and Frank Perdue were helping feed the New York City homeless. I overheard a bus driver who had transported the homeless children to the event cursing in front of them. I made a call to a source and got the driver's full name, date of birth, height, and weight. After checking further, I discovered that the driver had been imprisoned for rape and was using his brother's driver's license. The driver was immediately dismissed.

I went to speak with the executive director of The Children's Aid Society, Warren Moses, to introduce myself and to make him aware of the incident.

I was honored to have Warren Moses contact me shortly after that to work on behalf of The Children's Aid Society. I did pro-bono work for this charity for over 25 years, and this tremendous experience gave me the opportunity to be recognized as an Ellis Island Medal of Honor recipient.

In my eyes, children are like roses that bloom every day of the year.

FATHER WITH HEART

In 2000, I had the honor of meeting a giant of a man. This man had a huge heart. Not only was he devoted to his young daughter, but he had also proven to be, as a self-made man, a human with real compassion for others. This was an anomaly among powerful moguls.

It showed through his philanthropic work. It showed through his compassion to fund the rebuilding of a demolished city struck by natural disaster... and it showed in his passion for building business empires that would eventually make a whole industry thrive and offer enormous opportunities. There was just nothing superficial about this legend (whom we'll call "Heart" – I do not wish to name him). He was the real deal.

Heart hired my firm and me to work for him for what turned out to be, in an odd coincidence, 365 days in a row. There was another coincidence: The case happened to end on 9/11.

Our first meeting was at the Plaza Hotel. Heart's security man Steve joined us. Steve had been a sheriff in Las Vegas before being hired by Heart. I found him to have a very sharp mind and complete commitment to protecting his boss. We all spoke about life and our mutual love of boxing.

Heart had many past lives, and one of them was that of an amateur boxer. He'd scored 29 wins by knockout. He asked me if I wanted to "move around," meaning throw a few jabs circling one another. He was 83 at the time, and I was 20 years his junior. I guessed that he wanted to size me up. As Steve looked on, we had a few laughs. Nothing surprised him.

Ten years before meeting Heart, I was hired on the Mike Tyson/Robin Givens divorce case. At my first meeting with Tyson at Don King's Cleveland home, I remember asking him if he wanted to throw a few jabs at me. I shared the tale with my wife, Suzanne, and she went wild, though she seemed to have no problem with me "jabbing" with 83-year-old Heart years down the road.

Heart had hired us to protect his little girl, who we'll refer to as Amber. He loved Amber and wanted to take care of her, even though she wasn't his biological daughter.

There were some notable occurrences during the twelve months we worked for Heart. One particular day, a crazy New York City cab driver went over the curb in Central Park and barely missed hitting his daughter. Another time, in front of the Regency Hotel, I was walking with two of my investigators following Amber and her two nannies. Amber suddenly jumped into the street, right in front of the Irish doorman. The doorman swooped up the child within seconds before an impatient cabby nearly hit her pulling up to the curb.

We had to tell Heart of this incident because we were sure he'd find out. The next day, Heart asked me to have the doorman get us a cab. He wanted me to hand him five one-hundred-dollar bills. I commented to Heart that it might seem strange to the doorman to receive $500 as a tip for getting us a cab, but that was his kind and generous nature.

My favorite story was when Heart traveled by private plane. He always carried a gun. He had a gun-carrying license in many states, but not in New York City, which is one of the most difficult cities to get a permit. Since one of his best friends was the New York district attorney, he could always make a phone call for help. Heart called me one day to say that he left something in his hotel suite. He then asked me to pick up his .38-caliber, and that he'd collect it from me when he returned to New York the following week.

In those days, I carried my own .38. I was also the legal gun custodian for my investigators. You needed two separate licenses: one to carry a gun and one to be a custodian.

When I went to the high profile Fifth Avenue hotel, I assumed the security director was an ex-cop (which is usually the case). To cover myself, I called my legendary friend, Sal Blando, a retired captain of the police force. I asked Sal if he knew the security director of the hotel. Sal informed me that the hotel did not have a retired cop or FBI agent, just someone corporate. When I arrived, the security man was very nervous. I told him that I had come to retrieve a package that Heart had left in his suite. The security man, with his voice shaking, told me that it was a gun that Heart had left in the room, and he explained he couldn't give it to me. He instead intended to call one of the members of the board to discuss the matter.

I quickly showed the man my custodian gun license and asked him if he knew what the license was. I told him not to bother anyone and that I would sign for the gun and give him a copy of the license. I made a switch and gave him a copy of my P.I. License, not my gun custodian license. He never realized that my custodian license was only valid for my investigators. I guess he was not in school that day. When he handed me the gun, his hands were shaking. Heart had asked me to tip him $300, but I decided not to as it would appear we had done something wrong.

Life is very odd at times. In recounting this story to my family, I learned that Heart was a close friend of my father-in-law for many years. Heart died in 2015, at the age of 98. It seems there aren't many people like him around anymore.

THE FOOTMAN

When I was a teenager, my father, Frank Mullen, left the banking industry to become a private investigator. I started to help him out on cases as his "footman." Being a footman meant that you would follow a subject on foot while your partner drove the car. So, I became the footman for my dad and Charlie Lester, an outstanding licensed private investigator, and this was how I learned the trade. While my schoolmates were delivering pizzas or groceries, I was surveilling the sons or daughters of famous families.

After school, I would go home and dress up in my only suit and tie. Our neighbors in the Bronx would always ask me, "Who's getting married today?" I liked dressing nicely and learned that I could change up my look by simply wearing a different tie.

In about 1952 or 1953, my dad worked with legendary attorney John Broady at 19 Rector Street. Broady had been hired by a gentleman named O'Hara, who happened to be the patriarch of a prominent American family because he had a concern about his daughter. At the time, she was dating a famous actor, Dick Langley. O'Hara thought Langley might be gay, as he spent so much time with another attractive actor, Boz Quentin.

Lester and I had investigated Quentin months before. In that case, it turned out he had been sleeping with the wife of a prominent banker. I remember being impressed that Quentin would change his suits every three hours. He reminded me of James Mason, who was quite a debonair dresser.

We started the O'Hara case with surveillance at Quentin's apartment at 6 p.m. on a weekday. Quentin didn't leave his apartment until 9:30 p.m. I recall reminding Lester that I had to leave for school by 8:30 the next morning.

That was just the beginning of my taste for long hours, as Quentin and Langley would go out to all the clubs, dancing with the showgirls late into the night. I could always con my way into the clubs by saying that I was meeting my father, who was a judge, and that I needed to get the keys to our Park Avenue apartment. (The closest I would ever get to Park Avenue was serving a subpoena.)

Every night, Quentin and Langley would bring girls back to their apartment and party until 3 a.m. I was exhausted. Within three days I think I looked older than Lester, who was 30 years my senior.

As a result of our surveillance, Broady informed old man O'Hara that there was no way Langley could be gay – or a potentially faithful husband to his daughter. He and his friend chased beautiful women all over the city. In 1954, Langley married old man O'Hara's daughter. Twelve years on, with four children, their marriage was in divorce court.

In 1978, Quentin killed himself and his (younger) wife in an apartment building on West 57th Street. Maybe his heart had finally grown sensitive by the age of 65 after running around all of those years.

GPS

GPS—Global Positioning System—came out in the 1970s as the newest technology for the surveillance crowd: FBI, police, private investigators, and, unfortunately, stalkers. In our investigative work, we were using the satellite-based system for security and finding cheating spouses.

We had a case where an Upper East Side couple's nanny would take their baby in his carriage and disappear for a while. We put a GPS unit under the baby carriage, and the mother and father hoped it would show the nanny in Central Park on an innocent walk. Unfortunately, the nanny was found with the child at a West Side local watering hole. It turned out to be a short visit. The baby forgot to bring his I.D., and the nanny received a swift kick out the door.

Another case I'll never forget, and one I got a few white hairs over, was for a client who wanted her husband investigated because she suspected he was cheating on her. They were both Wall Street moguls, and every other day, it seemed, they appeared in the *New York Post's* Page Six column. She had top shelf attorneys with fancy Ivy League style.

We received a call from "Mrs. Mogul," who said her husband had decided to return his car to the rental company, but before that, he had to go to LaGuardia to pick up the leasing driver (who was returning the car). Her voice seemed strained. I called two of my investigators and had Investigator A track the male subject (our client's husband) from his computer at his home. He would then share the location of the subject with our Investigator B.

Investigator A shared that the male subject's car was in a West Side parking garage. Investigator B was getting into his car at his home upstate. We knew we had to remove the GPS from the subject's SUV before we missed our opportunity. My client's in-laws owned the leasing company, and if they found the GPS unit, they'd figure out that she was spying on her husband.

Since I was in Manhattan, I drove toward the parking garage. I got there while Investigator B was racing down from upstate to the airport to prepare himself for when the subject arrived.

When I entered the huge parking garage, the manager was standing right there, so I used an old trick.

"Hi," I said. "My uncle is in the hospital four blocks away...he's a cop from Midtown North." Then I whispered in the garage manager's ear, "His wife is still with him in his hospital room, and his girlfriend's panties and bra are in his trunk. But my uncle doesn't remember where he put the ticket or where he parked the car." The manager told me to go ahead and walk around to find the vehicle. I found the subject's SUV on the third floor. I got on my knees—the ground was about as clean as a slaughterhouse—and I started to reach under the back of the car when suddenly the car doors opened, and I could hear Mr. Mogul conversing with the garage attendant. Within a minute, they drove off while I was lying flat on the ground. A garage attendant walked over and said, "What did you lose?" I replied, "Only my dignity."

Investigator A continued to track the location of the male subject's SUV. He called and said that the SUV was going east towards LaGuardia. Investigator B told us he was stuck in traffic. By this time our client, who was following our trials and tribulations, was ready to go through the roof, afraid we would blow it. Since I could do nothing else to help, I went to wait at a favorite location for stressed detectives...my local Irish watering hole.

Investigator A tracked the SUV parked at LaGuardia in a specific parking lot while Investigator B was already on site. B went to the right terminal and finally located the subject's SUV on the fourth floor. The subject and the rental car driver had returned to the car and were talking. Investigator B "accidentally" dropped a handful of change on the ground right by the SUV as a decoy and started to pick the coins up. He grabbed the GPS unit, put it under his shirt, and then got the hell out of there.

We had spent hours of time on this and ended up getting the GPS unit within 20 seconds of the subject leaving.

Three months later, Page Six of the *New York Post* featured an item about Mr. & Mrs. Mogul finally getting a divorce.

HAITI, 1958

It was the late '50s and Papa Doc, a.k.a. François Duvalier, the president of Haiti, hired New York attorney John Broady for emergency help. Papa Doc was battling a Haitian civil war against the rebels. He was using his secret police, the Tonton Macoute, to fight this significant threat. The rebels were in the hills broadcasting a battle cry to the people of Haiti, "Get Papa Doc out!"

Papa Doc was his moniker because, before his rule, he had been a disease-fighting physician. Papa Doc, however, was never able to cure the ills of Haiti.

I was 23 and waiting for a second child at the time. Broady wanted my banker-turned-P.I. father and a genius electronics expert named George White to go to Haiti on his behalf. He told my dad to bring me along, but Dad was concerned about me leaving my young family, so I stayed behind.

George and Dad took the mission and flew to Haiti without knowing all the details. As they disembarked, a colonel and four uniformed men greeted them. Without warning, my dad was handed a .45-caliber pistol by the colonel. George was given a shotgun.

Dad and George turned to one another saying, "What the hell have we gotten ourselves into?"

They were also given an old automobile. All cars in Haiti were at least twenty years old, so they set up an antenna on the roof of the car and were followed by a bodyguard in a second car. It was their mission to find the rebels' broadcasting location. Luckily, there were no tourists due to the unrest of the war, and the streets didn't have their regular activity. Every night Dad called us in the Bronx to report the stories of the day. He recounted that Papa Doc had his own 1918 American tank from World War I that he had the soldiers drive around the National Palace as a sign of power and force. Dad said the tank had tremendous backfire because of their cheap oil. It was amusing to them.

One day, they sat down with President Duvalier, who asked my father, "Do you want a soda?" Dad was then shown the Coke machine and the technique for retrieving his drink, a swift kick. They got a real laugh out of that one.

One night the events were not so humorous.

Dad was in the local Police Department when a prisoner was brought in dressed only in underwear. The poor bloke had a beaten-up and bloodied face. There was a light hanging in the room, and the setting was very film noir—all mysterious shadows. They questioned the prisoner, and after about 10 minutes they dragged him out. Dad asked when his trial would be, and the colonel replied, "That was the trial."

After that, Dad stopped telling me his daily stories. All they wanted to do was to get the hell out of Haiti.

Finally, when they were eating a meal at a Port-au-Prince restaurant with the colonel and bodyguard, they had a rare chance to relax. At one point they stepped into the men's room to have a private conversation, and out of nowhere, the rebels launched a grenade into the bar, which blew the bodyguard's left leg off. Dad and George were on a plane before the leg hit the street!

Dad took photos and kept his passport close by to travel out of Haiti that night, and yes, they did leave the .45 and the shotgun behind. The next day they walked into Broady's office, and all they could say was, "You have to be kidding!"

Dad liked the Haitians very much. He felt they were smart and hard-working. He also said if you put twenty Haitians in a room and told them to pick a leader, you'd come back for the count, and there would be a list of twenty names, as they'd each vote for themselves.

Sixty years later, not much has changed for the poor Haitian people.

HEEEERE'S JOHNNY

Johnny Carson, the host of *The Tonight Show* from 1962 to 1992, was the true King of Comedy. There has never been another comedic host of late-night television quite like him.

As Carson became one of the most celebrated names in TV, he was having the time of his life dating and marrying numerous beautiful women. At times, he behaved like a college kid on a Fort Lauderdale spring break. Yet Carson was a very private, untrusting person, and he rarely engaged in idle conversation. Few understood just how complex a person he really was. Surprisingly, he didn't even hang out much with his partner on the show, Ed McMahon, or his musical conductor, Doc Severinsen.

Henry Bushkin, Johnny Carson's lawyer and confidant of 18 years, wrote a 300-page tell-all bestseller in 2013, simply titled, *Johnny Carson*. In the book, Bushkin references the now-famous 1970 "break-in."

"Bombastic Bushkin," as Carson dubbed him, assisted Carson in breaking into his wife's secret love pad in New York City. He and Carson got the keys to the apartment by greasing the palm of the building concierge's hand with a hundred bills.

While I was part of the team that helped Carson on this evening, I don't consider the event to be an actual break-in, as there were no locks, doors or windows broken.

After all, he was paying the bill for the place. I was relieved that he didn't see me pushing his wife's and her lover's undergarments under the sofa. He did, however, uncover what he had suspected, that the lover was none other than football great, Frank Gifford. It turned out to be a somber day for Carson.

On another night that I was called on to help out Carson, he had apparently made the moves on the wrong young woman. It was in his neighborhood bar that happened to be one of Frank Sinatra's favorite haunts, and this woman who had caught Carson's eye turned out to be the girlfriend of a very "well-connected" man.

His "boss" had graciously called a few burly guys over to the lounge to rough Carson up. I informed Bushkin that all of my men were unavailable to intervene, and my usual retired cops would not come out in the middle of the night.

The guys were hanging around, preventing Carson's exit, and trust me, they weren't there waiting to get his autograph. So I reached out to a congressman-friend who had been a police officer. He was able to influence the local precinct to dispatch a few uniformed cops to the bar, and they escorted Carson home, where he stayed holed up for three days. It turned out that there was a contract put out on his life. The New York City gossip pages wrote about Carson having the flu, making him unable to host *The Tonight Show* during that time.

In the years that followed, we did surveillance for Carson. One evening, we followed his wife, Joanne Carson, who was out with a famous South American singer. When we reported this back to Carson, he told us to cut the surveillance. He knew the man was gay.

There would never be a client like Carson nor a late-night host with his immense charm, wit, and intellect again.

HIGH SOCIETY SAGA

A New York high-society family, whom we'll call the Cassels, arrived in North America from Germany during the 1700s and made a name for themselves in business, social, and political circles in both the United States and the United Kingdom during the nineteenth and twentieth centuries.

In 1912, after an extended honeymoon to Egypt, then Paris, a young Catherine Juliane Cassel and Ralf Edgar Cassel IV were onboard the Titanic to return to the states. During the panic of the wreck, Catherine was assisted to a lifeboat by her husband, who didn't survive the fateful sinking of the newly christened steamship. Later that year, Catherine gave birth to their son (who she named after his father) and inherited her husband's fortune.

Several decades down the road, when I was a teenager, I worked with my dad and attorney John Broady. Broady happened to have done business with Ralf Edgar Cassel IV and his brother Walter Cassel.

Edgar Cassel IV was known to have spoiled women with lavish gifts.

At the time, a very wealthy, widowed socialite, who had once dated Edgar IV, brought to Broady a piece of jewelry for safekeeping. It was a massive diamond that had been given to her by Edgar IV. Broady assured the widow that her valued piece of jewelry would be well kept in the Cassel safe in a Jersey City bank.

Eventually, after Edgar IV had passed away, the widow and her attorney requested that Broady arrange an appointment for them to see her remarkable gem. Broady brought us along for the viewing. The widow's attorney had a diamond expert accompany them to examine the diamond for appraisal. After a tense, long silence, the appraiser broke the news that, in fact, the stone was not a valuable diamond at all, but merely a piece of cut crystal. If I recall correctly, the widow fainted right on the spot!

HIS MAJESTY KING HUSSEIN

My wife and I went to Scotland to see my relatives in the summer of 1997. Suzanne had a friend who had visited Inverlochy Castle and raved about it, so we made reservations to stay at the nearby luxury Inverlochy Castle Hotel located at the foot of the largest mountain, Ben Nevis.

Upon arrival at the airport, we rented a Mercedes SUV to drive to the hotel. We should have trained on the Formula One circuit before taking on the rugged Highland roads. It was very dangerous, and at one of the turns, we hit a rock wall and crushed a hubcap. As we got out to examine the damage, several Scottish residents stopped to help us. A lorry driver even asked if we wanted to follow him up to the castle.

We followed the lorry and arrived at the hotel to find beautiful architecture decorated with international flags, set within a majestic landscape. We were taken up wide stairways to our room. The castle hotel was built in 1863, and there were no elevators. As I relaxed, looking out of the windows at the landscape, I saw a helicopter within 150 feet of the castle. At that moment, the room phone rang, and the receptionist said, "We see your car has been hit, so we're changing your tire for you." I quickly went downstairs and saw a few men fixing my rental car's tire. I took note that they also had a security mirror to check under the auto for bombs. Within two minutes I just knew, because of my detective's mind, they were from Scotland Yard. By the third minute, I realized they were part of the security team for someone important. After talking to these agents, I gave them a copy of *Vendetta*, the Brian Burrough book that detailed our American Express investigation. One of the agents gave the book to His Majesty King Hussein of Jordan, a regular visitor there with Queen Noor and their children.

The next day, wandering the castle, I went into its grand library. I was mesmerized by the view of the rain out the window. I suddenly heard a man's voice behind me. "It's a great country, isn't it? The rain will eventually stop." I turned around, and it was King Hussein. We began to chat, and as I started to share with him that my mother was Scottish, his phone rang. He took the call and said, "King here." I began to laugh but put my hand over my mouth. He then put his hand over the phone to cover it, as he was laughing, too. We talked about life and Jordan's role within the area. I found this King to be a uniquely kind man.

The next day Suzanne and I went for a run in the misty rain. While we were returning on the road to the castle, two autos passed by. One was a Mercedes SUV similar to ours. His Majesty was driving with his bodyguard sitting next to him, and the Queen and her female attendant from Scotland Yard were in the back seat. The King opened the window and said, "So, do you Americans always run in the rain on Saturdays?" He was smiling.

"What does a King do on a Saturday?" I replied.

"Well, this King is taking his family to a Batman movie," he quipped, which made us all laugh. I later learned that the King flew his own helicopter while in Scotland. Just another thing that amazed me about this extraordinary man.

I decided to write to thank him for his kindness. He had his director, Brigadier Ali Shukri, write back to me within a very short time, inviting us to visit Amman, Jordan.

Great memories, a great soul, and indeed a great King.

A MARRIAGE, A MINISTER AND THE MAIL

Jerry Orbach was the King of Broadway and the Prince of TV. He was on the stage more than any other performer going back to Gilbert and Sullivan. Another actor said at his memorial, "Words cannot describe my feelings for Jerry Orbach. Let me just say that when I join him, I hope the things said about him can also be said about me. He was a perfect friend."

I was lucky enough to have had an office in the same high-rise with Jerry Orbach and his wife, Elaine, on the West Side. One day we happened to be getting our mail at the same time, and another tenant was there getting hers. She said to Jerry, "Oh, I see you got another letter from that nut, the minister."

I noticed the envelope appeared larger than usual, and its stamps were from the U.K., placed at the top right and running all the way down the side.

Orbach said to me, "Have I got a strange story for you, Joe."

The story went back to when Orbach lived with his first wife in Brooklyn, and they had a young neighbor who was getting married. She wasn't affiliated with a church nor did she have a fancy-enough home to hold her wedding. Orbach and his wife graciously offered to let her use their brownstone home for her big day. To know Jerry Orbach, you would expect nothing different.

Unfortunately, her groom—a young kid named Lombardo—turned out to be in the mob, later dying of lead poisoning from the bullets some enemy pumped into him. For years, people would ask Orbach what his relationship was with that young mobster Lombardo?

After the wedding, Lombardo's bride had apparently never paid the minister for his services. A few decades later, Orbach, who at this point was married to his second wife and living at a new address, started receiving collection letters from the minister demanding payment for that wedding day many years prior. These strange collection letters continued arriving for years. Orbach suspected that the minister must have spent at least a thousand dollars on stamps when the bride had owed him only four hundred.

On behalf of Orbach, I went out to Brooklyn to interview an elderly woman who was an old friend of the minister. I showed her my private investigator ID and explained to her that her friend had been harassing Jerry Orbach for many years, and could she please encourage him to stop?

Unfortunately, this elderly woman told the minister that Orbach had hired a private investigator to look into him and get him to behave. This fact seemed to delight the minister, and he continued to send the letters.

Finally, when Orbach couldn't take it anymore, he reached out to me again. I went to a Midtown precinct and filed a complaint called a "61" and sent a copy to the local North Yorkshire Police in the U.K. The constable went to the minister's home very late one night to get his attention. She told him to cease sending letters. However, all the minister wanted to know was who the private investigator was that Orbach had hired. The U.K. police constable realized he was ready to get more stamps for me! She somehow put a stop to that, and the letters to Orbach finally ceased.

Memories like these make me think what a great actor, singer, and wonderful person Jerry Orbach was. He indeed was a perfect friend.

NANNY FROM HELL

I worked for a very prominent New York governor who introduced me to a group of fine lawyers. Visiting their law firm was like walking into the Supreme Court. One day, one of the lawyers told me we were going to take on a job for a nurse who was being harassed by a middle-aged German nanny. I instantly wondered how in the world a nurse could afford these Wall Street attorneys.

The story was very odd. It seems the German nanny (who had cared for children from many of New York's socialite families) had gone to a Park Avenue doctor who resembled Cary Grant. The first time she laid eyes on this handsome doctor (we'll call him Dr. Grant), she was infatuated, even going so far as to unnecessarily take off her clothes for an exam. Soon she started making regular appointments with made-up illnesses so she could see the doctor.

Dr. Grant's nurse was our new client. She was also his secret girlfriend. The doctor had a lot going for him. He was a runner, an avid hunter, and an all-around nice, attractive guy.

It started with some gifts from the nanny, like silk ties from Brooks Brothers. At first, the doctor and the nurse thought it was cute. But when she kept the gifts coming and bought him expensive binoculars for hunting, they became somewhat concerned.

One day Dr. Grant was hunting in upstate New York, and as he rested his shotgun against a tree, something went horribly wrong, the gun misfired, and it took his head off.

That same weekend, the delusional nanny had made up wedding invitations for her imagined marriage to Dr. Grant and had even called the Pierre Hotel to schedule the wedding ceremony.

When the news broke about the accident, Dr. Grant's actual fiancée was devastated. The newspaper referred to her as the "bride to be" and colleague of Dr. Grant. This reality in the news was all the nanny needed to send her over the cliff.

At first, she started calling the nurse day and night. She had apparently stolen the nurse's contact information from the doctor's address book while in his office. She then started showing up at the nurse's apartment and wouldn't stop ringing her doorbell. Soon the envelopes came—plain white legal envelopes, which were filled with cockroaches, some still alive. The handwriting was a European style, and the nurse knew it was the nanny from hell.

Later, I learned from the attorney that one of the socialites got a few similar "letters" as well. Apparently, she had previously fired the nanny. The cockroach-filled envelope became the nanny's calling card.

The attorney made a complaint and got a subpoena for me to serve her. She lived in a third-floor walk-up on West End Avenue. The building had once been nice—maybe 20 years prior. We tried to call her before showing up, but her phone was out of order. We got information from a source at the telephone company that they had cut her phone line because six months before she had been harassing someone—namely, someone in New York society.

I slipped into the German nanny's building behind a tenant and walked up the three flights of stairs and knocked on her door. A woman whose hair and gaze looked like Big Foot's opened the door and saw I was standing there. She appeared to have been sleeping in her clothes for a week, too. I handed the subpoena to her, and she went nuts. I quickly exited down the three flights of stairs as she threw bags of garbage on me the whole way. I yelled up to her, "See you in court."

Just as I started to forget about the case, a lawyer called me from Greenwich, Connecticut, and told me the nanny didn't show up for her court date. Apparently, she had called the courts "from her bed" saying she had a bad foot. I suggested to him that this was highly unlikely since her phone service had been terminated. I then remembered there was a public phone on the street corner near her apartment.

I was given a second subpoena to serve her, this time from the judge. I went to the 20th Precinct and asked for a cop to accompany me because the subject was nuts. I didn't wear my best suit that day since she might give me another garbage shower. The precinct sent a patrolman along, and I gave him fair warning about her. I knocked on the door, and she quickly opened it without asking who it was.

She stared at the cop, looking right through me. She looked like a zany Phyllis Diller character doing her comedic schtick. She started screaming and yelling, then abruptly slammed the door. As the cop and I went down the stairs, we heard her banging on the door. I thanked the officer for his time, and we went in separate directions, laughing.

The subpoena I served her was for a hearing, where if charged, she could end up in the psych ward for 20 days. The other Park Avenue families also signed a complaint against her. I went to the courthouse for the trial and saw four major lawyers sitting in court. They had been hired by the "who's who" of the socialite scene. I was in the second row when the nanny limped in. To my surprise, she was elegantly dressed, resembling Grace Kelly. All the lawyers looked at me as if I was insane for describing her as a lunatic.

The judge started to ask the nanny questions, and her answers were like Shakespearean prose. Within ten minutes we were all looking at each other...thousands of dollars an hour spent, and the nanny from hell was breaking us. The socialites were scratching their well-groomed heads. I suddenly noticed her left shoe had a small hole cut in it, and a bandaged toe was peeking out. When the judge asked me to approach the bench, I walked up to her left side and stepped on her injured toe with all of my 190 pounds of weight. That was it. The honeymoon was over. Mrs. Frankenstein had arrived! She went completely ballistic. She was out of her mind yelling at the judge, at me, at the nurse, the correction officers, everyone.

The judge closed the hearing, and they took the nanny from hell off in handcuffs. As we all were leaving, the lead lawyer came up to me and said, "Great job. I've got a new case for you."

I replied, "No cockroaches, right?"

NIXON

In 1983, my wife and I began spending alternating weekends in Key Biscayne, Florida.

It also happened to be the location of what was President Nixon's "summer White House." The former president was a friend of Bebe Rebozo, a local banker I knew. He was also an avid fisherman, hiring my running buddy, Captain Jim O'Neil, to take him on fishing excursions down the key. One day when they were fishing, Nixon started to fall through the open end of the boat, and Jim saved him. Nixon, fortunately, had a light, humorous side and they laughed about it later over a few drinks.

I joined an old friend of mine, Nixon's chief operative, G. Gordon Liddy, to teach self-defense in Miami with our third partner, the bounty hunter Bob Burton. I taught the "Art of Surveillance."

I remember talking to President Nixon on an Eastern Airlines flight to New York about a strange attorney we both knew. Nixon said, "Keep a football field away from him." A passenger then interrupted us and asked him for his autograph. Then two more people came up and asked. He told the flight attendant to have all the people on board put their names on a large piece of paper. He took index cards and spent over an hour signing his name for everyone. I found this to be such a kind gesture.

In 1987, Nixon touched my family again. My youngest daughter had been diagnosed with a brain tumor. I did research to locate the best surgeon to perform her operation. The result was Dr. Malis at Mount Sinai Hospital. He was a pioneering innovator in micro-neurosurgery and renowned for inventing surgical instruments.

Unfortunately, when I called Malis's office, I was told he was on vacation. His secretary said she couldn't give us an appointment for several months. I had wrecked my office as a result of learning about my daughter's brain tumor. When I was straightening things back up later, I noticed a framed, signed letter from President Nixon. Without hesitation, I called Malis's office and told the nurse that I had forgotten to mention that President Nixon had recommended the neurosurgeon to me. The nurse asked me for my phone number and within ten minutes called back to tell me that Dr. Malis would see my daughter at 9 a.m. on the following Monday.

When I would see Dr. Malis, he never failed to ask me, "How is our president?" I started to feel guilty, so I wrote to President Nixon to confess. I told him that I had used our friendship and his name to get our doctor's appointment and that I was sorry. The next thing I knew, President Nixon sent a letter to Dr. Malis to thank him for helping my daughter. He also wrote a beautiful letter to my daughter.

Many years later, I was fortunate enough to help Mr. Nixon's grandson, Chris Cox, on a case, and my wife and I were invited to his wedding.

Nixon had a heart the size of his brain. Great man.

OTB

Years ago I had a client who spent much of his career in the medical field. He was excellent with numbers and developed an interest in the stock market and banking industry, and thus decided to change professions. He also had an interest in precious metals and had been collecting gold and silver, keeping most of what he'd purchased in his private vault.

My client embarked in private investing full time and succeeded quickly. He started an investment company and added salespeople to broker investments of other people's money as well. He expanded his business to Chicago and Los Angeles and began to travel and invest in real estate—eventually buying a private island.

This client was based in New York, and his company invested through both the New York and Chicago stock exchanges. Suddenly, some strange activity began happening in his Chicago office. His New York and Chicago offices worked together, but he always delegated and gave the directive to Chicago through his employees in New York.

At one point my client became suspicious of some activity in New York as well. Someone in one of the firms had invested in stocks from a company that my client knew was about to be taken over. He immediately called me to help him figure out the situation. I sat with him while he listened to some legally taped conversations held between the two offices. These tapes were made as an insurance policy in case an employee made an error of buying the wrong amount of a particular stock. He heard a conversation between brokers in the two offices and noticed that two specific men were repeatedly using a unique code. One of the brokers would often say, "Got it." When we reviewed a list of stocks, we realized that the men only used this code each time they discussed a stock from the company that was about to be taken over.

The client and I decided to conduct surveillance on his New York broker first. After following this young man for five days, we discovered he was going to Off Track Betting each day, sometimes twice a day. He would receive cash that had been deposited into his account and occasionally place a few bets.

My job was to help figure out how the two employees were able to split the profits of these particular stocks. I went to OTB and opened an account for myself and discovered that anyone could deposit cash into another person's account.

Bingo! We had our answer.

THE PATRIARCH

One of New York's finest divorce attorneys, Burton (Buddy) Monasch, left New York and moved to Los Angeles in the early 1980s to become the executive V.P. of Twentieth Century Fox. There he came to be regarded as one of the most prominent entertainment lawyers of that time. I was Buddy's private investigator for many years, and once he arrived in Hollywood, he introduced me to many movie stars and blue bloods of the industry.

One day very early on, Buddy told me that he had met with the son of a Hollywood legend. This star was a handsome leading man who always played the wealthy patriarch. In real life, he was the patriarch of his own large family, a devoted father and grandfather, and a true gentleman.

The son explained that his father was distraught. Apparently, his father had just returned from a college reunion in the Midwest that his manager had wanted him to attend as a P.R. stunt. After all those years, he recognized only four or five people at the event, but everyone lined up to greet him as if he were royalty. At the end of the evening, a woman came up to him. She was with a younger, middle-aged woman and introduced her to the star first. She then reached out her hand and said, "Do you remember me? We went on a few dates back in college." He didn't remember her but wanted to be pleasant, so he said, "Certainly, how are you doing?" They exchanged small talk, and as they were about to walk away from one another, the woman leaned over and whispered in his ear, "I'm glad you finally had the chance to meet your daughter." His knees buckled.

Later he spoke to the classmate who had organized the reunion and requested that he provide him with a list of everyone who had attended. He only remembered the woman's first name and picked out her and her daughter from the list. On his flight back to Los Angeles, he started to think about the episode. He recalled, during those years, that he had been quite a "player" and intimate with about half a dozen women.

His life had been out in the open ever since. Everyone knew he had made a fortune over the years and his new TV series was a success. The magazines had recently run photos of his family and grandchildren.

He began to worry that if this story came out, it would destroy his family, ruin his reputation, and have a disastrous effect on his career. He needed Buddy to make this go away.

Buddy called me and asked me to come to Twentieth Century Fox studios, which was a museum of stars, costumes, and movie sets. I left with information on the woman and her daughter: her home address, job, and personal information. Apparently, her husband had died in an accident two years before. I suspected now she needed money. After all, she was a grandmother whose daughter was divorced with three children of her own.

I immediately traveled to the small Midwestern town, leaving my best suits and ties behind and picking up a baseball cap from the local college bookstore. I rented a Jeep and drove to the older woman's home to observe. Within 15 minutes I realized she and her extended family all lived together. It was not like the *Beverly Hillbillies* exactly, but it was close. I was there to observe the lifestyle they led and to get the mother's and daughter's blood types. (After all, this was before DNA profiling came into play.)

There was a large tree with a tire swing hanging from it in the yard where the grandmother sat watching her grandchildren. It was Middle America and then some. Then I saw the daughter. She had one arm in a sling and bandages around her neck; she must have been in an accident. I drove two minutes to an intersection. I found the local bar, the dry cleaners, a flower shop and fancy new drugstore, like one would see on New York City's Madison Avenue. I went to the bar and spoke to the bartender on a ruse. I told him some gal who had on bandages and a sling had given me directions to the bar. He said, "Oh Mary! She had a bad accident down the street about a month ago."

I downed my glass of wine and then called Buddy and brought him up to date. The fact that the drugstore that seemed to be state of the art, and the only one within 50 miles, led me to tell him that we might get lucky on the case.

Next, I approached the drugstore's owner, introduced myself using my I.D. and told him I was on the trail of a con woman who had, over time, stolen half of a million dollars. Skeptical, the owner asked why I chose to come to his drugstore?

I explained that the con woman had made calls from a particular phone number, which happened to be his public phone booth. I also said to him, "Did I tell you this woman I'm searching for has an illness, and she apparently needs a blood supplement?" The owner then allowed me to search his three-by-five index cards and within minutes, I found the records of the two women. I discovered that the younger woman's blood type was different and that she could not be the movie star's daughter.

Sometime after, I started to watch the star's TV series. I recalled the whole case, and I realized Buddy had been the real star, though I didn't complain. I had gotten well paid, too!

PRINCES OF THE CATHOLIC CHURCH

I've had the personal pleasure of getting to know three cardinals of the New York Catholic Church.

As a young man, my father, Frank Mullen, introduced me to Cardinal Francis Spellman at Our Lady of Refuge in the Bronx. Cardinal Spellman, though cherubic in appearance, was a ruthless player on the world stage. Spellman was a complex individual and wielded a large amount of power. He was a first-rate fundraiser and a brilliant businessman. When he died in 1967, President Lyndon Johnson, Vice President Hubert Humphrey, New York Senators Robert Kennedy and Jacob Javits and Governor Nelson Rockefeller attended his funeral. His 28-year tenure as archbishop is the longest to date in the history of the Archdiocese of New York.

My closest, lifelong friend, Congressman Mario Biaggi, introduced me to Cardinal John O'Connor, as they had developed a great friendship. Cardinal O'Connor, a towering presence, was a leader who forcibly injected his views and personality into the great civic debates of his time. He became one of the Catholic Church's most potent symbols on moral and political issues.

I recall joining Mario in a St. Patrick's Day Mass. Mario sat alongside Cardinal O'Connor in one of the two huge chairs placed at the entranceway to St. Patrick's Cathedral. In the past, during the St. Patrick's Day ceremonies, the Cardinal would stand and walk the 80 feet to Fifth Avenue to greet the mayor of New York City. (The New York mayor would always use the St. Patrick's Day Parade for political reasons.) Cardinal O'Connor knew that Mayor Giuliani was not a friend of Mario Biaggi's, and, in fact, had been instrumental in prosecuting and imprisoning Biaggi. I watched as the cardinal did not greet Giuliani, as was the custom. He instead stayed in his chair waiting for the mayor to approach him. While the cardinal was holding Mario's left hand, Giuliani kissed the ring on the cardinal's right hand. Cardinal O'Connor's bodyguard, a New York City cop, a young priest, and I all stood close by amazed at the Cardinal's gesture of loyalty for Mario Biaggi. Who was it that said, "Church and state do not mix"?

I also met Cardinal Timothy Dolan, the current Archbishop of New York, when attending a Police Athletic League charity luncheon.

We instantly hit it off that day, becoming friends. Cardinal Dolan had an incredible sense of humor evidenced not only in a letter he sent me saying, "Dear Joe, you are my unofficial Swiss Guard," but also telling me funny stories over lunch. The best was when his mother learned that he was to be appointed archbishop of New York, she said, "Ah dear... now your cardinal uniform will hide that large stomach of yours!"

We had a good laugh.

THE ROOSEVELT JR. YEARS

My father had three older aunts who worked on Wall Street. They were all progressives and real characters, very much like Auntie Mame. They retired fairly young and together moved to Pawling, New York, in Dutchess County. The home they bought was the style of a big farmhouse, set on dozens of acres. They were board members for the National Bank of Pawling, and being Republicans, they had gotten to know Governor Tom Dewey, who also lived in Pawling. Just over the hill in Poughkeepsie, along Route 9, was President Roosevelt's Hyde Park summer home. The Roosevelts were the Royal Family of Dutchess County. For years, I had no idea my aunts knew them.

One cold fall day, I went to Clove Creek Farm located in Poughkeepsie on a case. I looked up at this tall man. His face was his dad's face, and right then and there I knew I was looking at history. (As a kid, I only knew my president was Roosevelt and that the heavyweight boxing champ was Joe Louis.) Franklin D. Roosevelt Jr. and I had a conversation ... one of many over the years. That day, we chatted for half an hour about family and the area. I had remarked to FDR Jr. how cold it was, and he replied, "Well, at least the horses love it." We both laughed. He told me to hold on so he could get me a cup of coffee before we got down to business. He brought back a hot mug, the size of a football, with a large handle on it. It looked like a stein. I asked him if he had any cream and he told me, "Real men drink coffee black. Besides, if you're going to be driving back on the dark Dutchess County roads, that coffee will keep you awake." He was right. I was awake for the next 36 hours. It was the strongest coffee I had ever had.

While I was there, the phone rang, and he picked it up and said, "Hi, General." He started to tell the General why I had come to see him. I could tell the person he was talking to was in Washington, D.C., and I suddenly realized who the person on the other end of the line was. He was one of the most powerful men in our government. FDR Jr. was asking the General to help him deport a South American horseman that he had regretted hiring.

Jr. said to the General, "I need another cup of coffee. Speak to Joe the P.I. from New York City." I took the phone, and the General's first words were, "Is he drinking?" I said yes, but just atomic-strength coffee. I said that my left arm had gone completely numb from it, which made him laugh.

After a long conversation, the General told me, "Joe, you now have to do your thing; I can't get involved." I promised him I'd do a full investigation. The next day, the General was in the papers about important government matters.

Throughout the '80s, FDR Jr. gave me a half of a dozen cases, and we became friends.

One day he called me because he wanted to talk about investing in more fine race horses like the Whitney's. The problem was he didn't want to spend vast amounts for them. He then told me he was soon going to Saratoga with a new horse that came from a "strong bloodline." I asked him what he was talking about, and he said, "I just bought a colt for a fair price in New Jersey and his father was a champion. I sent you a Federal Express package with a copy of a magazine with an old horse on the cover. That's my new colt's father."

Something tugged at my mind about this, and I had an uneasy hunch. I called him back and asked if he had paid for the new colt. He said he had and that he'd already mailed the check. So I drove with an ex-detective to the horse farm in New Jersey. It was huge and had a separate employee entrance. A smart businessman had opened a bar just 15 feet away from that entrance, and naturally, all the employees of the farm hung out there. It had an old neighborhood bar feel with a phone booth in the parking lot out front.

The ex-detective and I arrived separately. We sat three seats from one another so we could get others into a conversation, which was an old detective trick, as was chatting with the bartender, which I did. I held the horse magazine with the colt's striking father on the cover. A groomer sat down between my partner and me and asked if he could read my magazine. I hesitated just as the groomer looked down and said in his Spanish accent, "Wow, my God, we have one of his colts here on the farm." I said he must be a breathtaking horse! The groomer replied, "No, unfortunately, he's ill with stomach cancer. I don't think he will make it to autumn."

I rushed to the phone booth. FDR Jr. picked up, and I screamed, "Cancel the check!"

As we left the bar, the bartender said to me, "Hey, you claimed you live in Key Biscayne, but you left me two subway tokens." I said, "I guess you didn't know we built a subway there."

We all laughed.

ROY COHN

Roy Cohn was one of the most controversial figures of the twentieth century. Sidney Zion described him in his 1988 book, *The Autobiography of Roy Cohn*, as the toughest gay man in America.

His friends considered him a compatriot, a loyal pal, a fearless attorney. He was also one of the greatest party throwers—unparalleled in New York society. His enemies knew him as a native fascist, a brainy Joe McCarthy. He was the legal executioner of Ethel and Julius Rosenberg. Behind the scenes, he was the evil genius lawyer for J. Edgar Hoover, Cardinal Spellman, and the Mafia, and an advisor to Richard Nixon and Ronald Reagan.

Sidney Zion was one of my drinking buddies. We used to meet up at Kennedy's on West 57th Street. Very few friends could keep up with Sidney except for Steve Dunleavy, the great *New York Post* columnist. Sid wrote on the jacket of his book he gave me: "Dear Joe, if Roy had had you in his corner, this book would not have been necessary."

A major New York attorney who was a friend of mine had asked me to arrange to have Roy Cohn's garbage picked up at his East Side townhouse at night. I drove by the townhouse and observed that the amount of trash left at curbside was enough to fill a Pennsylvania mine shaft! We hired two employees from our building's private garage to take Cohn's trash away on a wooden flatbed truck.

Our investigators monitored our guys collecting Cohn's trash, always in the middle of the night. Every so often there were people out on the street who observed them, so when this happened, our hired guys would collect the garbage of the adjacent townhouses as well. This activity went on for quite a while.

It dawned on me that we might be pushing our luck doing this for months on end, as Cohn had some tough Mafia friends.

One day while going through the trash, we found a letter from a private garbage company who supposedly serviced Roy Cohn's townhouse. It stated that they wanted to increase his fees due to the excessive volume of garbage they had to pick up. We laughed to ourselves—this company hadn't picked up Roy Cohn's garbage for at least a year. We had!

Only in America.

ROUNDTABLE

I used to take a daily run in Central Park. Each day, heading back to my office, I would stop at Carnegie Deli.

There was a daily roundtable set up, though it was not to be confused with that of King Arthur. One might say it was a "salami table."

The group of roundtable regulars included the Broadway writer and critic Jack O'Brien, opera singer Bob Merrill, Leo Steiner, the co-owner of the establishment, and comedian and violinist Henny Youngman, who was famous for his one-liners. I was a regular at the table.

Every time comedians were in town, they'd sit down with us. I remember Norman Crosby, Joan Rivers, Howie Mandel, and Jackie Mason joining us, too.

Henny would say, "Chicken." Then he'd tell a joke about a chicken. The next person would take the lead, and for 20 minutes jokes were shared about "chicken." Even the waiter would get in on the act.

Henny would also tell his favorite joke each day. "What did you do yesterday?" he'd say as if asking himself. Then he'd reply, "I took a pleasure trip ... I took my mother-in-law to the airport." It was usually the high point of my day, and I'd laugh all the way back to my office.

One day, Jack O'Brien said to me, "Joe, I got a call from Ralph Bellamy, you know, the very classy actor." Ralph told Jack that a great American actor/dancer was being taken advantage of by his caregivers. Apparently, the female caregiver was married to the actor's accountant. The caregiver and accountant had taken over the actor's estate. Like many stars, even today, their homes, autos, boats, etc., are under their corporation's name. I did some research, and it turned out that the accountant had opened a company with a similar name to that of the unwitting actor in his care (i.e., The Kelly Inc. instead of The Kelly Co.). So when the actor's payments came in from the shows and movies he appeared in, much of that money was stolen and funneled to the fake account of his thieving caregivers.

No one went to jail for this. Life is not always fair. I loved this star and still watch him in old movies today.

SPY WORLD

For many years, we've used the services of The Spy Store in New York City. The owner, Bob Leonard, is a retired police officer and Marine. When working with our clients, there is usually need to do a "sweep" of the subject's premises, which is how we find out if there are any recording devices on the phones, in the car, or anywhere in the home.

One of our cases involved an international banker who arranged to fly Leonard and me on his private plane to his private island, where we proceeded to do a full sweep of his computers, phones, homes, garages, tennis courts, automobiles, etc. What we uncovered was that the banker's security people had bugged his entire property. There were recording devices everywhere, even in his private library.

We left the island and Leonard, and I listened to the tapes from each of the bugs removed from the island. One thing we found was that our client had unwittingly paid all the hospital bills for the wife of one of his security detail.

After informing our client, he decided to play a trick on his employees, whom he felt he could trust before. He made up a story about a company that his bank was about to take over and leaked the tip. As a result of his set up, these men invested heavily in the so-called bank take over and lost all of their investments.

The client alerted the local district attorney to the facts behind our sweep, as well as the insider tip that was used as a set-up against his greedy security people.

Another case involved a socialite who maintained a beautiful garden at her European home. She was weeding in her garden one day and was pulling up a root. It turned out the root had gotten entwined with a wire coming from her bedroom. Someone had installed a video camera in her bedroom and had hidden the cables in her garden. The socialite's home sat on the top of a hill, so when the local police walked the grounds with me, we followed the wiring directly down to a neighbor who was a bizarre, eccentric character. This person ended up being convicted in the U.K. and was sent to prison for a little vacation.

With most of our cases, we recommend The Spy Store to our clients, impressing the importance of videos and other paraphernalia to help them with their security issues. For example, video cameras and GPS units were always helpful for parents checking on the nanny, a wife suspicious of her husband's activities, or a father wondering where the teenage son goes in the middle of the night. One can even travel with a video in a camera to leave in a hotel room to make sure the housekeeper is only cleaning the room. The CIA, FBI, Homeland Security, MI-6, KGB, and, naturally, 007 use all of these tools of the trade.

TAKE ME OUT TO THE BALL GAME

I had the pleasure of meeting an icon through a close mutual friend. This man was the owner of one of America's top baseball teams. I remember the first thing he had said to me was to call him Karl.

Throughout the 1980s and '90s, I did a dozen investigations for his team.

In one case, Karl had paid handsomely to sign a particular top pitcher. During the very first day of spring training, this pitcher hurt his shoulder, which naturally made Karl furious. He was convinced the pitcher had arrived with the injury, so he asked me to travel to the Midwest town of the player to investigate. I remember driving along the wheat fields, just waiting for a young Judy Garland and her little dog to run into the road.

I finally arrived in the pitcher's farm town. It was classic like an old movie set, with one car mechanic's garage, one bar, one grocer, one drug store, a sheriff's office, and a high school with a baseball field.

Some of the props I brought along included letters addressed with similar names to the famous pitcher. I walked into the drug store and headed for the phone booth. I placed a call to the phone company, which gave me the number from which I was calling. I used this phone to open a conversation with the pharmacist. I told him that we had traced the phone number to his phone booth. As I wanted to get information from him, I made up a story about a "wanted man" who had used this particular phone many times. I also told him we knew that the man was abusing prescription drugs. I explained that we were searching for information that could be helpful, and I requested that the pharmacist allow me to look at his drug registry for the wanted man's name and address.

As a seasoned investigator I had used this ruse many times, and fortunately, it paid off again. The pharmacist showed me the registry that listed the drugs he had been prescribing the pitcher. The drugs consisted of numerous pain medications.

I went to the local bar to find out more info about the pitcher. Since I was paying for everyone's drinks, I learned that the pitcher was a local hero and that everyone knew all about his recent tractor accident, which had ripped open his shoulder. I didn't even bother to open my overnight bag. I returned to New York immediately to write up the report.

I had another case concerning Karl's team. It was a hot summer day, and the papers had reported that a woman, who was seated in the stadium with her husband and two children, had been shot. A witness was quoted as saying that the kids were eating hot dogs and had mustard all over their hands. The woman was reaching in her bag for some napkins when a shot rang out.

The press mistakenly reported that someone in the neighborhood was firing shots from a rooftop. Obviously, Karl was very concerned that the public would be afraid to come to more home games if there was dangerous gunfire around his stadium.

We uncovered a few things. First, that the woman's husband was an IRA member, and second, that she was carrying a gun in her pocketbook and accidentally hit the trigger while she was fishing for the napkins and shot herself.

I went to the bar that this IRA member frequented with some of my investigators for a drink. There was a picture of Margaret Thatcher on the wall, and the patrons were throwing darts at her face. As we left, one of the female customers walked ahead of us and turned around. To our surprise, she lifted her blouse up, and she wasn't wearing a bra. Needless to say, my men and I didn't fit that bar scene.

Karl and I shared some good laughs about that one.

TALENT IS A GIFT FROM GOD

I worked with a sports and entertainment attorney over the years. Most of our cases related to famous athletes who had incidents such as DWIs or fighting with a current girlfriend (usually a model) at some trendy bar.

Inevitably, the *New York Post's* gossip column, Page Six, would cover the details, highlighting the woman's beautiful legs or the "it" people she had just traveled with to St. Barts. The hired PR would protect their client from any real embarrassment.

We always kept our eyes on the ball, protecting the athlete, as we knew the lawsuits would follow.

In one instance, we helped the attorney with one of his favorite basketball players. The star himself had not done anything wrong, but he had a relative—a hanger-on type—who hit a woman over the head with a phone. Our client calmed the waters by buying the victim a beautiful home to "help her move on."

Then there was the mega singing star and her crazy husband. He had his wife locked up in their mansion and was keeping her from speaking to the attorney. I had two ex-cops join us, and together with the attorney, we drove to Greenwich, Connecticut, to try to talk with them. The husband, a talentless musician, struggling to survive, apparently had his own bodyguards who were street thugs from the old hood, and they carried guns that were likely not registered.

I had advised the attorney that the two ex-cops accompanying us could not, by law, carry their guns in the state of Connecticut. (This had not been the case before 9/11.)

We arrived at the palatial estate where there was a large courtyard in front of the home's entranceway. We observed the crazy, shirtless husband glaring out of one of the front windows. The sequestered singer was waving to us from the third-floor balcony.

The attorney rang the front door several times and then started banging. Finally, the irate husband opened the door, and none of us expected what we witnessed. He was standing there completely naked except for a gun belt with guns in the two holsters. He had a joint hanging from his lips, and he looked completely stoned. Before the attorney had a chance to say anything, a school bus pulled into the courtyard. The couple's two children jumped off the bus as their mother made her escape through the housekeeper's entrance to greet them. She had an overnight bag with her, and she swiftly moved the children to the attorney's car.

After an altercation with the stoned husband, we managed to get out of there. We stopped at a drive-thru to get food for the kids. The husband would probably be coming after us if only he could get his pants on. Our client told us that he'd not be following at all. She had taken the keys to their three cars. On top of that, he had recently been arrested for a DWI, so he would only be able to follow us in a limo that would never get to their home in time.

Talent may be a gift from God, but fame can lead to delusion. Common sense, however, shows you the way out of the woods when life becomes complicated.

WHAT HAPPENS IN VEGAS

A prestigious matrimonial attorney called me. This lawyer's client was a relative of an Arab nation leader. He explained that this gentleman, who we'll call Ahmad, had three children; the youngest was age 4, and the twins, age 7. His wife, Amelle, wanted a divorce but feared she wouldn't get a fair hearing in their country, so she fled with the children.

She had run away with not only the children but also bags of cash and jewelry. The value of the jewels could keep her living like a queen, even if she survived to be 100. Since her name would obviously be familiar to the border guards, she went through Israel, where both countries have agreements. It became a political storm. The Arab leader was outraged. Ahmad was a far better parent than Amelle, who had battled drug addiction. His attorney achieved sole custody for Ahmad very quickly.

At one time, the couple had lived in Manhattan, and Amelle had a good friend who adored their kids. She was like an aunt to them. If anyone knew where Amelle and her children had gone, it would be her.

We started researching the friend first. We found that she lived in a high-rise building very familiar to us. We waited until it was the week of the twins' birthday and watched as they came and went. Amelle knew that Ahmad would search the cell phone bills and credit card charges, but she didn't expect he'd think about her friend.

Meanwhile, we needed more information, so we got a garbage truck to pick up all the trash from the apartment building. I hired two off-duty garbage men to pick up the garbage twice that week. We had an enormous wooden table set up in a West Side garage and had the men going through everything—no easy task. After several hours, we had learned a few things; we knew a man on the third floor was having affairs and the superintendent was a drunk. Then we hit pay dirt. We discovered UPS receipts from Amelle's friend addressed to Las Vegas. They showed what we presumed to be Amelle's Vegas apartment address and phone number.

Ahmad was ready. He ordered a private plane; we were going to leave from an airport in New Jersey. I asked a weightlifter to accompany us as extra muscle.

I was packed, and before I left, my wife said, "I hope you're doing the right thing. They're her children, too." It ruined my flight.

We arrived in Vegas. Our room was reserved under the weightlifter's name, Tony. The apartment Amelle was renting looked like a motel and was located behind a huge casino. They were on the third floor. When the apartment door was open, it faced the walkway so we could see her, but she could not see us. Ahmad was now wearing a hairpiece and a phony mustache. I couldn't laugh in front of him, but he looked pretty funny.

On the second day, we saw her hand in hand with, presumably, a new boyfriend. He appeared to be a Native American. What bothered us was that he was with three other men and was bossing them around. It seemed he was the chief and everyone else served as her bodyguards.

The first day of school, they all came out of the motel—the Native Americans had their own rooms. The three bodyguards and the boyfriend drove the children to school with their mother. We followed them to the school, which had a large yard with a wire fence around it. We had to practically sit on top of Ahmad to stop him from running out screaming for his kids. He almost blew our cover the first day. By this time, we were calling him "Elvis," but never to his face.

We kept watch and saw after ten minutes that the children had been separated. The twins were taken to a different building than the four-year-old, who was in preschool. That could be a problem. Also, there was no gate for the father to get into the yard. He grew exceedingly nervous. Things got tougher for Ahmad as the boyfriend waited with Amelle until the children went into their classrooms. They then left, with Tony on their tail, and went to the local coffee shop.

I went to the hardware store to buy wire cutters and clear tape. We returned to the school and found that the bodyguards were still there. We also took note of some heavy "casino hitters" who had armed bodyguards for their children as well.

We left the school, stopping at the coffee shop where we knew they had gone. We had bought locks for the two large glass doors. We planned to lock them inside and flatten their tires.

But they weren't all there, so we held off, as we didn't want another Custer battle.

Later that night, Tony cut a four-foot-by-four-foot door in the wire fence and taped it shut. You couldn't see it unless you were standing two feet away. The next day we left with our bags, hoping our "Vegas vacation" would soon be over. "The best laid plans of mice and men," as they say...

Finally, on the third day, the boyfriend accompanied the kids and bodyguards to school wearing a bowie knife on his belt. "Great," I said to Ahmad. "We'll let him take your fake rug." We had arrived before them. They parked their station wagon a block away, and we sat in our throwaway rental where Ahmad laid in the backseat. After the children were dropped off, all four of them went to the usual coffee shop to eat. Tony flattened their tires; then we called him to let him know all three kids were in the yard and that Dad was going through the fence. I told him to lock the two coffee shop doors pronto and catch up with us! Ahmad ran across the field yelling his children's names, and the kids started to run toward him. We were concerned because some of the teachers were running towards us. The kids and Dad (minus his rug, which had fallen off) jumped into the car with us.

We caught up with Tony near the highway. He had left the throwaway car with a sign saying "dead battery." We started going to a private airport and heard on the radio that an incident happened at the school. Tony called the rental agency and told them that one of the cars had broken down and the other was left at the airport. The radio was telling a story of kids who were kidnapped. I told Ahmad to tell his lawyer to call the local police NOW. The kids were all over him, so elated, and we were in the air within 40 minutes, en route back to New York City.

Many years later, the father introduced me to the twins, who were then in college. It was a happy ending!

WE DID NOT CHOOSE OUR GRANDSON

A white-glove law firm called me to help them with an important client. (The Ivy League bus must have left its campus and made this firm its first stop.)

The attorney who called was a good guy with a great sense of humor...one not necessarily needed, however, in a case with a ridiculous subject, such as this one.

The lawyer's client was a prominent member of a large American family with a certain highbrow notoriety. His 28-year-old grandson was in trouble with the law. The problem had begun the year before we were hired when the family's trust invested in a Fifth Avenue condo for $20 million. They had let the dubious grandson reside there.

This kid was not your typical tenant. It seems he had been bringing prostitutes into the apartment night and day. The local police were ready to set up shop in the lobby of the building since they were being called almost daily by the condominium's board.

The board members (whose ages averaged around 70) were now evicting the grandson after only a year.

On one particular weekend, the grandson had invited a prostitute to his apartment for an extended stay. When he escorted the woman to her limo on Sunday night, he had nothing on except his underwear, and cocaine was found inside the elevator and all over his condo. When scrutinized, the grandson told the lawyer that his guest had partied with him the entire weekend and had brought with her a hand-held credit card machine to get paid. She charged his American Express card every twelve hours. Little did the kid realize that the total came to $80,000. He tried to explain his way out of it by insisting that the prostitute had worked very hard to earn the money...as if this would excuse things.

The lawyer insisted that the grandson relinquish the prostitute's agency information so we could secure the backup receipts since the family's trust was paying the bill. We I.D.'d the phone number, then contacted our friend Sal Blando, the former captain of the 19th Precinct, to accompany us on the house call.

The lawyer told us that because the prostitute had not collected the entire amount from the American Express transactions, we should do our best to cancel the unprocessed receipts.

Sal and I went on a little visit to the agency. The office was in a walk-up. We rang the bell and were invited up to the third floor. When we entered, we were standing in a one-room studio about the size of John Gotti's cell. The middle-aged woman in charge was not attractive and obviously not a working girl, just a bookkeeper of sorts. When we asked her what line of work she was conducting there, she replied that she was in the public relations business. We inquired what kind of PR her employee had done for $80,000 throughout the weekend prior. I noticed that she was staring at Sal Blando's diamond-encrusted captain's ring. She nervously told us that she had not yet put through every charge on the credit card, but remarked that her young PR associate was very professional and a hard worker. She was resisting as we pushed her to cancel the unprocessed charges. It was like asking a divorce attorney to return part of his retainer fee. Finally, we were successful and ripped up $35,000 worth of receipts.

I called the grandson and told him how lucky he was that we were able to confiscate $35,000 worth of his irresponsible purchases, and all he could ask was, "Is my friend mad at me?" My reply to the kid was "his friend" had just earned $15,000 a day. What did he think?

Sal and I laughingly agreed that we were clearly in the wrong business.

Made in the USA
San Bernardino,
CA